Politically
Correct
Bedtime
Stories

Politically Correct Bedtime Stories

*Expanded edition
with a new story:*
'Pinocchio'

James Finn Garner

SOUVENIR
PRESS

First published in Great Britain in 1994 by
Souvenir Press,
an imprint of Profile Books Ltd
29 Cloth Fair
London
EC1A 7JQ
www.profilebooks.co.uk

This expanded edition, with a new story, 'Pinocchio', first published 2021

First published in the United States by
Macmillan Publishing Company, New York

An excerpt originally appeared in *Playboy* magazine

Copyright © 1994, 2011, 2021 by James Finn Garner

Illustrations by Lisa Amoroso

3 5 7 9 10 8 6 4 2

Printed and bound in Great Britain by Clays Ltd, Elcograf S.p.A.

A CIP catalogue record for this book is available from the British Library.

ISBN 978 1 78816 513 6

FSC
www.fsc.org
MIX
Paper from
responsible sources
FSC® C018072

To the Theater of the Bizarre,
including Pepe, Armando, Egon, Ted,
Matteo, Nick and Julietta; James Ghelkins Jr,
and Willie, Smitty and Jocko
of the Teamsters Children's Puppet Theater;
and Others too numerous to mention.
To Carol, for help and encouragement,
and to Lies, for everything.

Contents

Introduction

I t's been a quarter-century since my first processed tree carcass was published, in an effort
to improve the world by rethinking the biases
baked into children's stories. The idea was simple:
smash the patriarchy by smashing the patriarchs of
bedtime, like the Siblings Grimm and mer-misogy-
nist Hans Christian Andersen.

It's a good time to take stock of our successes.
Anti-wolf bias is declining, Prince Charmings are
being exposed for their stalkerish ways, and formerly marginalised trolls have enjoyed a stunning
comeback, thanks to the Internet.

Yet the world is still afflicted by backward thinking and so many regressive ills. I don't know what
else to do, except release this book again, this time
with bonus material. Commercial? Certainly, but
sometimes you have to use the system to upend
the system. We will not get (sorry for this ethnic

insensitivity) a Mulligan for our lives here. This is the only earth we have on this planet, and bedtime remains the best time to save it.

Little Red Riding Hood

here once was a young persun named Red Riding Hood who lived with her mother on the edge of a large wood. One day her mother asked her to take a basket of fresh fruit and mineral water to her grandmother's house – not because this was womyn's work, mind you, but because the deed was generous and helped engender a feeling of community. Furthermore, her grandmother was *not* sick, but rather was in full physical and mental health and was fully capable of taking care of herself as a mature adult.

So Red Riding Hood set off with her basket through the woods. Many people believed that the forest was a foreboding and dangerous place and never set foot in it. Red Riding Hood, however, was confident enough in her own budding sexuality that such obvious Freudian imagery did not intimidate her.

On the way to Grandma's house, Red Riding Hood was accosted by a wolf who asked her what was in her basket. She replied, 'Some healthful snacks for my grandmother, who is certainly capable of taking care of herself as a mature adult.'

The wolf said, 'You know, my dear, it isn't safe for a little girl to walk through these woods alone.'

Red Riding Hood said, 'I find your sexist remark offensive in the extreme, but I will ignore it because of your traditional status as an outcast from society, the stress of which has caused you to develop your own, entirely valid, world view. Now, if you'll excuse me, I must be on my way.'

Red Riding Hood walked on along the main path. But, because his status outside society had freed him from slavish adherence to linear, Western-style thought, the wolf knew a quicker route to Grandma's house. He burst into the house and ate Grandma, an entirely valid course of action for a carnivore such as himself. Then, unhampered by rigid, traditionalist notions of what was masculine or feminine, he put on Grandma's nightclothes and crawled into bed.

Red Riding Hood entered the cottage and said, 'Grandma, I have brought you some fat-free, sodium-free snacks to salute you in your role of a wise and nurturing matriarch.'

From the bed, the wolf said softly, 'Come closer, child, so that I might see you.'

Red Riding Hood said, 'Oh, I forgot you are as optically challenged as a bat. Grandma, what big eyes you have!'

'They have seen much, and forgiven much, my dear.'

'Grandma, what a big nose you have – only relatively, of course, and certainly attractive in its own way.'

'It has smelled much, and forgiven much, my dear.'

'Grandma, what big teeth you have!'

The wolf said, 'I am happy with *who* I am and *what* I am,' and leaped out of bed. He grabbed Red Riding Hood in his claws, intent on devouring her. Red Riding Hood screamed, not out of alarm at the wolf's apparent tendency towards cross-dressing, but because of his wilful invasion of her persunal space.

Her screams were heard by a passing

woodcutter-persun (or log-fuel technician, as he preferred to be called). When he burst into the cottage, he saw the melee and tried to intervene. But as he raised his axe, Red Riding Hood and the wolf both stopped.

'And just what to you think you're doing?' asked Red Riding Hood.

The woodcutter-persun blinked and tried to answer, but no words came to him.

'Bursting in here like a Neanderthal, trusting your weapon to do your thinking for you!' she exclaimed. 'Sexist! Speciesist! How dare you assume that womyn and wolves can't solve their own problems without a man's help!'

When she heard Red Riding Hood's impassioned speech, Grandma jumped out of the wolf's mouth, seized the woodcutter-persun's axe, and cut his head off. After this ordeal, Red Riding Hood, Grandma and the wolf felt a certain commonality of purpose. They decided to set up an alternative household based on mutual respect and cooperation, and they lived together in the woods happily ever after.

The Emperor's New Clothes

ar away, in a time long past, there lived a travelling tailor who found himself in an unfamiliar country. Now, tailors who move from place to place normally keep to themselves and are careful not to overstep the bounds of local decency. This tailor, though, was overly gregarious and decorum-impaired, and soon he was at a local inn, abusing alcohol, invading the persunal space of the female employees and telling unenlightened stories about tinkers, dung-gatherers and other tradespeople. The innkeeper complained to the police, who grabbed the tailor and dragged him in front of the emperor. As you might expect, a lifetime of belief in the absolute legitimacy of the monarchy and in the inherent superiority of males had turned the emperor into a vain and wisdom-challenged tyrant. The tailor noticed these traits and decided to use them to his advantage.

The emperor asked, 'Do you have any last request before I banish you from my domain for ever?'

The tailor replied, 'Only that your majesty allow me the honour of crafting a new royal wardrobe. For I have brought with me a special fabric that is so rare and fine that it can be seen only by certain people – the type of people you'd want to have in *your* realm – people who are politically correct, morally righteous, intellectually astute, culturally tolerant, and who don't smoke, drink, laugh at sexist jokes, watch too much television, listen to country music or barbecue.'

After a moment's thought, the emperor agreed to this request. He was flattered by the fascist and testosterone-heavy idea that the empire and its inhabitants existed only to make him look good. It would be like having a trophy wife and multiplying that feeling by 100,000.

Of course, no such rarefied fabric existed. Years of living outside the bounds of normal society had forced the tailor to develop his own moral code that obliged him to swindle and embarrass the emperor

in the name of independent craftspeople every-
where. So, as he diligently laboured, he was able
to convince the emperor that he was cutting and
sewing pieces of fabric that, in the strictest objec-
tive sense of reality, didn't exist.

When the tailor announced that he was finished,
the emperor looked at his new robes in the mirror.
As he stood there, naked as the day he was born,
one could see how years of exploiting the peasantry
had turned his body into an ugly mass of puffy white
flesh. The emperor, of course, saw this too, but pre-
tended that he could see the beautiful, politically
correct robes. To show off his new splendour, he
ordered a parade to be held the next day.

On the following morning, his subjects lined the
streets for the big parade. Word had spread about
the emperor's new clothes that only enlightened
people with healthy lifestyles could see, and everyone was determined to be more right-minded than
his or her neighbour.

The parade began with great hoopla. As the
emperor marched his pale, bloated, patriarchal
carcass down the street, everyone loudly oohed and
aahed at his beautiful new clothes. All except one
small boy, who shouted, 'The emperor is naked!'

The parade stopped. The emperor paused. A hush fell over the crowd, until one quick-thinking peasant shouted, 'No, he isn't. The emperor is merely endorsing a clothing-optional lifestyle!'

A cheer went up from the crowd, and the throngs stripped off their clothes and danced in the sun, as nature had intended. The country was clothing-optional from that day forward, and the tailor, deprived of any livelihood, packed up his needle and thread and was never heard from again.

The Three Little Pigs

nce there were three little pigs who lived together in mutual respect and in harmony with their environment. Using materials that were indigenous to the area, they each built a beautiful house.

One pig built a house of straw, one a house of sticks, and one a house of dung, clay and creeper vines shaped into bricks and baked in a small kiln. When they were finished, the pigs were satisfied with their work and settled back to live in peace and self-determination.

But their idyll was soon shattered. One day, along came a big, bad wolf with expansionist ideas. He saw the pigs and grew very hungry, in both a physical and an ideological sense. When the pigs saw the wolf, they ran into the house of straw. The wolf ran up to the house and banged on the door, shouting, 'Little pigs, little pigs, let me in!'

The pigs shouted back, 'Your gunboat tactics hold no fear for pigs defending their homes and culture.'

But the wolf wasn't to be denied what he thought was his manifest destiny. So he huffed and puffed and blew down the house of straw. The frightened pigs ran to the house of sticks, with the wolf in hot pursuit. Where the house of straw had stood, other wolves bought up the land and started a banana plantation.

At the house of sticks, the wolf again banged on the door and shouted, 'Little pigs, little pigs, let me in!'

The pigs shouted back, 'Go to hell, you carnivorous, imperialistic oppressor!'

At this, the wolf chuckled condescendingly. He thought to himself, *They are so childlike in their ways. It will be a shame to see them go, but progress cannot be stopped.*

So the wolf huffed and puffed and blew down the house of sticks. The pigs ran to the house of bricks, with the wolf close at their heels. Where the house of sticks had stood, other wolves built a time-share resort complex for holidaying wolves, with each unit a fibreglass reconstruction of the house of sticks, as well as native curio shops, snorkelling and dolphin shows.

At the house of bricks, the wolf again banged on the door and shouted, 'Little pigs, little pigs, let me in!'

This time in response, the pigs sang songs of solidarity and wrote letters of protest to the United Nations.

By now the wolf was getting angry at the pigs' refusal to see the situation from the carnivore's point of view. So he huffed and puffed, and huffed and puffed, then grabbed his chest and fell over dead from a massive heart attack brought on from eating too many fatty foods.

The three little pigs rejoiced that justice had triumphed and did a little dance around the corpse of the wolf. Their next step was to liberate their homeland. They gathered together a band of other pigs who had been forced off their lands. This new brigade of *porcinistas* attacked the resort complex with machine guns and rocket launchers and slaughtered the cruel wolf oppressors, sending a clear signal to the rest of the hemisphere not to meddle in their internal affairs. Then the pigs set up a model socialist democracy with free education, universal health care and affordable housing for everyone.

Please note: The wolf in this story was a metaphorical construct. No actual wolves were harmed in the writing of the story.

Rumpelstiltskin

ong ago in a kingdom far away, there lived a miller who was very economically disadvantaged. This miller shared his humble dwelling with his only daughter, an independent young wommon named Esmeralda. Now, the miller was very ashamed of his poverty, rather than angry at the economic system that had marginalised him, and was always searching for a way to get rich quick.

'If only I could get my daughter to marry a rich man,' he mused in a sexist and archaic way. 'She'll be fulfilled and I'll never have to work another day in my life.' To this shabby end, he had an inspiration. He would start a rumour that his daughter was able to spin common barnyard straw into pure gold. With this untruth, he would be able to attract the attention of many rich men and marry off Esmeralda.

The rumour spread throughout the kingdom in a manner that just happened to be like wildfire and soon reached the prince. As greedy and gullible as most men of his station, he believed the rumour and invited Esmeralda to his castle for a May Day festival. But when she arrived, he had her thrown into a dungeon filled with straw and ordered her to spin it into gold.

Locked in the dungeon, fearing for her life, Esmeralda sat on the floor and wept. Never had the exploitativeness of the patriarchy been made so apparent to her. As she cried, a diminutive man in a funny hat appeared in the dungeon.

'Why are you crying, my dear?' he asked.

Esmeralda was startled but answered him: 'The prince has ordered me to spin all this straw into gold.'

'But why are you crying?' he asked again.

'Because it can't be *done*. What are you, specially abled or something?'

The differently statured man laughed and said, 'Dearie, you are thinking too much with the left side of your brain, you are. But you are in luck. I will show you how to perform this task, yes, but first you must promise to give me what I want in return.'

With no alternative, Esmeralda gave her assent. To turn the straw into gold, they took it to a nearby farmers' cooperative, where it was used to thatch an old roof. With a drier home, the farmers became healthier and more productive, and they brought forth a record harvest of wheat for local consumption. The children of the kingdom grew strong and tall, went to a cooperative school, and gradually turned the kingdom into a model democracy with no economic or sexual injustice and low infant mortality rates. For his part, the prince was captured by an angry mob and stabbed to death with pitchforks outside the palace. As new investment money poured in from all over the world, the farmers remembered Esmeralda's generous gift of straw and rewarded her with numerous chests of gold.

When all this was done, the diminutive man in the funny hat laughed and said, '*That* is how you turn straw into gold.' Then his expression became menacing. 'Now that I have done my work, you must fulfil your part of the bargain. You must give me your first-born child!'

Esmeralda shot back at him, 'I don't have to negotiate with anyone who would interfere with my reproductive rights!'

The vertically challenged man was taken aback by the conviction in her voice. Deciding on a change in tactics, he said slyly, 'Fair enough, dearie. I'll let you out of the bargain if you can guess what my name is.'

'All right,' said Esmeralda. She paused a second, tapped her chin with her finger and said, 'Would your name be ... oh, I don't know, maybe ... Rumpelstiltskin?'

'AAAAAKKKK!!' shrieked the man of non-standard height. 'But ... but ... how did you know?'

She replied, 'You are still wearing your name badge from the Little People's Empowerment Seminar.'

Rumpelstiltskin screamed in anger and stamped his foot, at which point the earth cracked open and swallowed him up in a rush of smoke and sulphur. With her gold, Esmeralda moved to California to open a birth-control clinic, where she showed other womyn how not to be enslaved by their reproductive systems and lived to the end of her days as a fulfilled, dedicated single persun.

The Three Codependent Goats Gruff

nce on a mountainside lived three goats who were related as siblings. Their name was Gruff, and they were a very close family. During the winter months they lived in a lush, green valley, eating grass and doing other things in a naturally goatish manner. When summer came, they would travel up the mountainside to where the pasture was sweeter. This way, they did not overgraze their valley and kept their ecological footprints as small as possible.

To get to this pasture, the goats had to cross a bridge over a wide chasm. When the first days of summer came, one goat set out to cross the bridge. This goat was the least chronologically accomplished of the siblings and thus had achieved the least superiority in size. When he reached the bridge, he lashed on his safety helmet and grasped the handrail. But as he began to cross, a menacing growl came from beneath the bridge.

Over the railing and on to the bridge leaped a troll – hairy, dirt-accomplished and odour-enhanced. 'Yaaarrrgh!!' intoned the troll. 'I am the keeper of this bridge, and while goats may have the right to cross it, I'll eat any that try!'

'But why, Mr Troll?' bleated the goat.

'Because I'm a troll, and proud of it. I have a troll's needs, and those needs include eating goats, so you better respect them or else.'

The goat was frightened. 'Certainly, sir,' he stammered. 'If eating me would help you become a more complete troll, nothing would please me more. But I really can't commit to that course of action without first consulting my siblings. Will you excuse me?' And the goat ran back to the valley.

Next, the middle sibling goat came up to the bridge. This goat was more chronologically advanced than the first goat and so enjoyed an advantage in size (although this did not make him a better or more deserving goat). He was about to cross the bridge when the troll stopped him.

'Nature has made me a troll,' he said, 'and I embrace my trollhood. Would you deny me my right to live the life of a troll as fully and effectively as I can?'

'Me? Never!' exclaimed the goat proudly.

'Then stand still there while I come over and eat you up. And don't try to run away; I would take that as a persunal affront.' He began to invade the goat's caprinal space.

'However,' blurted the goat, 'I have a very close family, and it would be selfish of me to allow myself to be eaten without asking their opinion. I have respect for their feelings too. I would hate to think that my absence would cause them any emotional stress, if I hadn't first—'

'*Go* then!' screamed the troll.

'I'll rush back here as soon as we reach a consensus,' the goat said, 'for it's not fair to keep you in suspense.'

'You're too kind,' sighed the troll, and the goat ran back to the valley. As his hunger grew, the troll began to feel a real grievance towards the goats. If he didn't get to eat at least one of them, he was determined to go to the authorities.

When the third goat came to the bridge, the troll discovered that he was nearly twice the troll's size, with large, sharp horns and hard, heavy hooves. The troll felt his physical-intimidation prerogative fading fast. As fear turned his insides into jelly, the troll sank to his knees and pleaded, 'Oh, please, please forgive me! I was using you and your goat siblings for my own selfish ends. I don't know what drove me to it, but I've seen the error of my ways.'

The goat, too, got down on what passed for knees in goats and said, 'Now, now, you can't take all the blame for yourself. Our presence and supreme edibility put you in this situation. My siblings and I all feel terrible. Please, *you* must forgive *us*.'

The troll began to sob. 'No, no, it's all my fault. I threatened and bullied you all, just for the sake of my own survival. How selfish I was!'

But the goat would have none of this. 'We were the selfish ones. We only wanted to save our own skins, and we totally neglected your needs. Please, eat me now!'

'No,' the troll said, 'you must butt me off this bridge for my insensitivity and selfishness.'

'I'll do no such thing,' said the goat, 'since we all tempted you in the first place. Here, have a chomp. Go ahead.'

'I'm telling you,' the troll insisted, standing up, 'I'm the guilty one here. Now, knock me off this bridge and be quick about it!'

'Look,' said the goat, rearing to his full height, 'no one is going to take away my blame for this, not even you, so eat me before I pop you in the nose.'

'Don't play guiltier-than-thou with me, Hornhead!'

'"Hornhead"? You smelly hairball! I'll show you guilt!' And with that, they wrestled and bit and punched and kicked as each sought to don the mantle of blame.

The other two goats bounded up to the bridge and sized up the fight. Feeling guilty at not accepting enough of the blame, they joined the others in a whirling ball of hair, hooves, horns and teeth. But the little bridge was not built to carry such weight. It shook and swayed and finally buckled, hurling the troll and the three codependent goats Gruff into the chasm. On their way down, they each felt relieved that they would finally get what they deserved, plus, as a bonus, a little extra guilt for the fate of the others.

Rapunzel

here once lived an economically disadvantaged tinker and his wife. His lack of material accomplishment is not meant to imply that all tinkers are economically marginalised, or that if they are, they deserve to be so. While the archetype of the tinker is generally the whipping persun in classic bedtime stories, this particular individual was a tinker by trade and just happened to be economically disadvantaged.

The tinker and his wife lived in a little hovel next to the modest estate of a local witch. From their window, they could see the witch's meticulously kept garden, a nauseating attempt to impose human notions of order on to nature.

The wife of the tinker was pregnant, and as she gazed at the witch's garden, she began to crave some of the lettuce she saw growing there. She begged the tinker to jump the fence and get some for her. The tinker finally submitted, and at night he jumped the wall and liberated some of the lettuce. But before he could get back, the witch caught him.

Now, this witch was very kindness-impaired. (This is not meant to imply that all, or even some, witches are that way, nor to deny this particular witch her right to express whatever disposition came naturally to her. Far from it, her disposition was without doubt due to many factors of her upbringing and socialisation, which, unfortunately, must be omitted here in the interest of brevity.)

As mentioned earlier, the witch was kindness-impaired, and the tinker was extremely frightened. She held him by the scruff of the neck and asked, 'Where are you going with my lettuce?'

The tinker might have argued with her over the concept of ownership and stated that the lettuce rightfully 'belonged' to anyone who was hungry and had nerve enough to take it. Instead, in a degrading spectacle, he pleaded for mercy. 'It was my wife's fault,' he cried in a characteristically male manner.

'She is pregnant and has a craving for some of your lovely lettuce. Please spare me. Although a single-parent household is certainly acceptable, please don't kill me and deprive my child of a stable, two-parent family structure.'

The witch thought for a moment, then let go of the tinker's neck and disappeared without a word. The tinker gratefully went home with the lettuce. A few months later, and after agonising pain that a man will never really be able to appreciate, the tinker's wife gave birth to a beautiful, healthy prewommon. They named the baby Rapunzel, after a type of lettuce.

Not long after this, the witch appeared at their door, demanding that they give her the child in return for the witch having spared the tinker's life in the garden. What could they do? Their powerless station in life had always left them open to exploitation, and this time they felt they had no alternative. They gave Rapunzel to the witch, who sped away.

The witch took the child deep into the woods and imprisoned her in a tall tower, the symbolism of which should be obvious. There Rapunzel grew to wommonhood. The tower had no door or stairs, but it did boast a single window at the top. The only way for anyone to get to the window was for Rapunzel to let down her long, luxuriant hair and to climb it to the top, the symbolism of which should also be obvious.

The witch was Rapunzel's only companion. She would stand at the foot of the tower and shout,

'Rapunzel, Rapunzel, let down your hair,
That I might climb your golden stair.'

Rapunzel obediently did as she was told. Thus for years she let her body be exploited for the transportational needs of another. The witch loved music and taught Rapunzel to sing. They passed many long hours singing together in the tower.

One day a young prince rode near the tower and heard Rapunzel singing. But as he rode closer to find the source of the lovely sound, he spied the witch and hid himself and his equine companion in the trees. He watched as the witch called out to Rapunzel, the hair fell down, and the witch climbed up. Again, he heard the beautiful singing. Later, when the witch finally left the tower and disappeared in the other direction, the prince came out of the woods and called up,

'Rapunzel, Rapunzel, let down your hair,
That I might climb your golden stair.'

The hair cascaded from the window, and he climbed up.

When the prince saw Rapunzel, her greater-than-average physical attractiveness and her long, luxuriant hair led him to think, in a typically lookist way, that her persunality would also be beautiful. (This is not to imply that all princes judge people solely on their appearance, nor to deny this particular prince his right to make such assumptions. Please see the disclaimers in the paragraphs above.)

The prince said, 'Oh, beautiful damsel, I heard you singing as I rode by on my horse. Please sing for me again.'

Rapunzel didn't know what to make of this persun, since she had never seen a man up close before. He seemed a strange creature – large, hairy in the face, and possessing a strong, musky odour. For reasons she could not explain, Rapunzel found this combination somewhat attractive and opened her mouth to sing.

'Stop right there!' screamed a voice from the window. The witch had returned!

'How . . . how did you get up here?' Rapunzel asked.

'I had an extra set of hair made, in case of emergency,' said the witch matter-of-factly. 'And this certainly looks like one. Listen to me, Prince! I built this tower to keep Rapunzel away from men like you. I taught her to sing, training her voice for years. She'll stay here and sing for no one but me, because I am the only one who truly loves her.'

'We can talk about your codependency problems later,' said the prince. 'But first let me hear – Rapunzel, is it? – let me hear Rapunzel sing.'

'NO!' screamed the witch. 'I'm going to throw you from the tower into the thorn-of-colour bushes below so that your eyes will be gouged out and you'll wander the countryside cursing your bad luck for the rest of your life!'

'You may want to reconsider that,' said the prince. 'I have some friends in the recording industry, you see, who would be very interested in . . . Rapunzel, wasn't it? Different, kind of catchy, I suppose . . .'

'I knew it! You want to take her from me!'

'No, no, I want you to continue to train her, to nurture her . . . as her *manager*,' said the prince. 'Then, when the time is right, say a week or two, you can unleash her talent on the world and we can all rake in the cash.'

The witch paused for a second to think about this, and her demeanour visibly softened. She and the prince began to discuss record contracts and video deals, as well as possible marketing ideas, including life-like Rapunzel™ dolls with their very own miniature stereo Tune-Towers™.

As Rapunzel watched, her suspicions turned into revulsion. For years her hair had been exploited for the transportational needs of others. Now they wanted to exploit her voice as well. *So, rapaciousness does not depend solely on gender*, she realised with a sigh.

Rapunzel edged her way to the window without being seen. She stepped out and climbed down the second set of hair to the prince's waiting horse. She dislodged the hair and took it with her as she rode off, leaving the witch and the prince to argue about royalties and percentages in their phallus-shaped tower.

Rapunzel rode to the city and rented a room in a building that had real stairs. She later established the non-profit Foundation for the Free Proliferation of Music and cut off her hair for a fundraising auction. She sang for free in coffee houses and art galleries for the rest of her days, always refusing to exploit for money other people's desires to hear her sing.

Cinderella

here once lived a young wommon named Cinderella, whose natural birthmother had died when Cinderella was but a child. A few years after, her father married a widow with two older daughters. Cinderella's mother-of-step treated her very cruelly, and her sisters-of-step made her work very hard, as if she were their own persunal unpaid labourer.

One day an invitation arrived at their house. The prince was celebrating his exploitation of the dispossessed and marginalised peasantry by throwing a fancy-dress ball. Cinderella's sisters-of-step were very excited to be invited to the palace. They began to plan the expensive clothes they would use to alter and enslave their natural body images to emulate an unrealistic standard of feminine beauty. (It was especially unrealistic in their case, as they were differently visaged enough to stop a clock.) Her mother-of-step also planned to go to the ball, so Cinderella was working harder than a dog (an appropriate if unfortunately speciesist metaphor).

When the day of the ball arrived, Cinderella helped her mother- and sisters-of-step into their ball gowns. A formidable task: it was like trying to force ten pounds of processed nonhuman animal carcasses into a five-pound skin. Next came immense cosmetic augmentation, which it would be best not to describe at all. As evening fell, her mother- and sisters-of-step left Cinderella at home to finish her housework. Cinderella was sad, but she contented herself with her Holly Near records.

Suddenly there was a flash of light, and in front of Cinderella stood a man dressed in loose-fitting, all-cotton clothes and wearing a wide-brimmed hat. At first Cinderella thought he was a Southern lawyer or a bandleader, but he soon put her straight.

'Hello, Cinderella, I am your fairy godpersun, or individual deity proxy, if you prefer. So, you want to go to the ball, eh? And bind yourself into the male

CINDERELLA

concept of beauty? Squeeze into some tight-fitting dress that will cut off your circulation? Jam your feet into high-heeled shoes that will ruin your bone structure? Paint your face with chemicals and make-up that have been tested on nonhuman animals?'

'Oh yes, definitely,' she said in an instant. Her fairy godpersun heaved a great sigh and decided to put off her political education till another day. With his magic, he enveloped her in a beautiful, bright light and whisked her away to the palace.

Many, many carriages were lined up outside the palace that night; apparently, no one had ever thought of car-sharing. Soon, in a heavy, gilded carriage painfully pulled by a team of horse-slaves, Cinderella arrived. She was dressed in a clinging gown woven of silk stolen from unsuspecting silkworms. Her hair was festooned with pearls plundered from hard-working, defenceless oysters. And on her feet, dangerous though it may seem, she wore slippers made of finely cut crystal.

Every head in the ballroom turned as Cinderella entered. The men stared at and lusted after this wommon who had captured perfectly their Barbie-doll ideas of feminine desirability. The womyn, trained at an early age to despise their own bodies, looked at Cinderella with envy and spite. Cinderella's own mother- and sisters-of-step, consumed with jealousy, failed to recognise her.

Cinderella soon caught the roving eye of the prince, who was busy discussing jousting and bear-baiting with his cronies. Upon seeing her, the prince was struck with a fit of not being able to speak as well as the majority of the population. *Here*, he thought, *is a wommon that I could make my princess and impregnate with the progeny of our perfect genes, and thus make myself the envy of every other prince for miles around. And she's blonde too!*

The prince began to cross the ballroom towards his intended prey. His cronies also began to walk towards Cinderella. So did every other male in the ballroom who was younger than seventy and not serving drinks.

Cinderella was proud of the commotion she was causing. She walked with head high and carried herself like a wommon of eminent social standing. But soon it became clear that the commotion was turning into something ugly, or at least socially dysfunctional.

The prince had made it clear to his friends that he was intent on 'possessing' the young wommon.

But the prince's resoluteness angered his pals, for they too lusted after her and wanted to own her. The men began to shout and push each other. The prince's best friend, who was a large if cerebrally constrained duke, stopped him halfway across the dance floor and insisted that *he* was going to have Cinderella. The prince's response was a swift kick to the groin, which left the duke temporarily inactive. But the prince was quickly seized by other sex-crazed males, and he disappeared into a pile of human animals.

The womyn were appalled by this vicious display of testosterone, but try as they might, they were unable to separate the combatants. To the other womyn, it seemed that Cinderella was the cause of all the trouble, so they encircled her and began to display very unsisterly hostility. She tried to escape, but her impractical glass slippers made it nearly impossible. Fortunately for her, none of the other womyn were shod any better.

The noise grew so loud that no one heard the clock in the tower chime midnight. When the bell rang the twelfth time, Cinderella's beautiful gown and slippers disappeared, and she was dressed once again in her peasant's rags. Her mother- and sisters-of-step recognised her now, but kept quiet to avoid embarrassment.

The womyn grew silent at this magical transformation. Freed from the confinements of her gown and slippers, Cinderella sighed and stretched and scratched her ribs. She smiled, closed her eyes and said, 'Kill me now if you want, sisters, but at least I'll die in comfort.'

The womyn around her again grew envious, but this time they took a different approach: instead of exacting vengeance on her, they stripped off their bodices, corsets, shoes and every other confining garment. They danced and jumped and screeched in sheer joy, comfortable at last in their shifts and bare feet.

Had the men looked up from their macho dance of destruction, they would have seen many desirable womyn dressed as if for the boudoir. But they never ceased pounding, punching, kicking and clawing each other until, to the last man, they were dead.

The womyn clucked their tongues but felt no remorse. The palace and realm were theirs now. Their first official act was to dress the men in their discarded dresses and tell the media that the fight arose when someone threatened to expose the cross-dressing tendencies of the prince and his cronies. Their second was to set up a clothing co-op that produced only comfortable, practical clothes for womyn. Then they hung a sign on the castle advertising CinderWear (for that was what the new clothing was called), and through self-determination and clever marketing, they all – even the mother- and sisters-of-step – lived happily ever after.

Goldilocks

hrough the thicket, across the river, and deep, deep in the woods, lived a family of bears – a Papa Bear, a Mama Bear and a Baby Bear – and they all lived together anthropomorphically in a little cottage as a nuclear family. They were very sorry about this, of course, since the nuclear family has traditionally served to enslave womyn, instil a self-righteous moralism in its members and imprint rigid notions of heterosexualist roles on to the next generation. Never the less, they tried to be happy and took steps to avoid these pitfalls, such as naming their offspring the non-gender-specific 'Baby'.

One day, in their little anthropomorphic cottage,

they sat down to breakfast. Papa Bear had prepared big bowls of all-natural porridge for them to eat. But straight off the stove, the porridge was too thermally enhanced to eat. So they left their bowls to cool and took a walk to visit their animal neighbours.

After the bears had left, a melanin-impoverished young wommon emerged from the bushes and crept up to the cottage. Her name was Goldilocks, and she had been watching the bears for days. She was, you see, a biologist who specialised in the study of anthropomorphic bears. At one time she had been a professor, but her aggressive, masculine approach to science – ripping off the thin veil of nature, exposing its secrets, penetrating its essence, using it for her own selfish needs and bragging about such violations in the letters columns of various magazines – had led to her dismissal.

The rogue biologist had been watching the cottage for some time. Her interest was to collar the bears with radio transmitters and then follow them in their migratory and other life patterns, with an utter disregard for their persunal (or rather, animal) privacy. With scientific espionage the only thing in mind, Goldilocks broke into the bears' cottage. In the kitchen, she laced the bowls of porridge with a tranquillising potion. Then, in the bedroom, she rigged snares beneath the pillows of each bed. Her plan was to drug the bears and, when they stumbled into their bedroom to take a nap, lash radio collars to their necks as their heads hit the pillows.

Goldilocks chortled and thought, *These bears will be my ticket to the top! I'll show those twerps at the university the kind of guts it takes to do* real *research!* She crouched in a corner of the bedroom and waited. And waited, and waited some more. But the bears took so long to come back from their walk that she fell asleep.

When the bears finally came home, they sat down to eat breakfast. Then they stopped.

Papa Bear asked, 'Does your porridge smell . . . off, Mama?'

Mama Bear replied, 'Yes, it does. Does yours smell off, Baby?'

Baby Bear said, 'Yes, it does. It smells sort of chemical-y.'

Suspicious, they rose from the table and went into the living room. Papa Bear sniffed. He asked, 'Do you smell something else, Mama?'

Mama Bear replied, 'Yes, I do. Do you smell something else, Baby?'

Baby Bear said, 'Yes, I do. It smells musky and sweaty and not at all clean.'

They moved into the bedroom with growing alarm. Papa Bear asked, 'Do you see a snare and a radio collar under my pillow, Mama?'

Mama Bear replied, 'Yes, I do. Do you see a snare and a radio collar under my pillow, Baby?'

Baby Bear said, 'Yes, I do, and I see the human who put them there!'

Baby Bear pointed to the corner where Goldilocks slept. The bears growled, and Goldilocks awoke with a start. She sprang up and tried to run, but Papa Bear caught her with a swing of his paw, and Mama Bear did the same. With Goldilocks now a mobility non-possessor, Mama and Papa Bear set on her with fang and claw. They gobbled her up, and soon there was nothing left of the maverick biologist but a bit of yellow hair and clipboard.

Baby watched with astonishment. When they were done, Baby Bear asked, 'Mama, Papa, what have you done? I thought we were vegetarians.'

Papa Bear burped. 'We are,' he said, 'but we're always ready to try new things. Flexibility is just one more benefit of being multicultural.'

Snow White

nce there was a young princess who was not at all unpleasant to look at and had a temperament that many found to be more pleasant than most other people's. Her nickname was Snow White, indicative of the discriminatory notions of associating pleasant or attractive qualities with light, and unpleasant or unattractive qualities with darkness. Thus, at an early age, Snow White was an unwitting if fortunate target for this type of colourist thinking.

When Snow White was quite young, her mother was suddenly stricken ill, grew more advanced in non-health, and finally was rendered non-viable. Her father, the king, grieved for what can be considered a healthy period of time, then asked another wommon to be his queen. Snow White did her best to please her new mother-of-step, but a cold distance remained between them.

The queen's prized possession was a magic mirror that would answer truthfully any question asked it. Now, years of social conditioning in a male hierarchical dictatorship had left the queen very insecure about her own self-worth. Physical beauty was the one standard she cared about now, and she defined herself solely in regard to her persunal appearance. So every morning the queen would ask her mirror,

'Mirror, mirror, on the wall,
Who's the fairest one of all?'

Her mirror would answer,

'For all it's worth, O my queen,
Your beauty is the fairest to be seen.'

That dialogue went on regularly until once when the queen was having a bad-hair day and was desperately in need of support, she asked the usual question and the mirror answered,

'Alas, if worth be based on beauty,
Snow White has surpassed you, cutie.'

At this the queen flew into a rage. The chance to work with Snow White to form a strong bond of sisterhood had long passed. Instead, the queen indulged in an adopted masculine power trip and ordered the royal woodspersun to take Snow White into the forest and kill her. And, possibly to impress the males in the royal court, she barbarously ordered that the girl's heart be cut out and brought back to her.

The woodspersun sadly agreed to these orders, and led the girl, who was now actually a young wommon, into the middle of the forest. But his connections to the earth and seasons had made him a kind soul, and he couldn't bear to harm the girl. He told Snow White of the oppressive and unsisterly order of the queen and told her to run as deeply as she could into the forest.

The frightened Snow White did as she was told. The woodspersun, fearing the queen's wrath but unwilling to take another life merely to indulge her vanity, went into town and had the confectioner concoct a heart of red marzipan. When he presented this to the queen, she hungrily devoured the heart in a sickening display of pseudo-cannibalism.

Meanwhile, Snow White ran deep into the woods. Just when she thought she had fled as far as she could from civilisation and its unhealthy influences, she stumbled upon a cottage. Inside she saw seven tiny beds, set in a row and all unmade. She also saw seven sets of dishes piled high in the sink and seven reclining chairs in front of seven remote-controlled TVs. She surmised that the cottage belonged to either seven little men or one sloppy numerologist. The beds looked so inviting that the tired youngster curled up on one and immediately fell asleep.

When she awoke several hours later, she saw the faces of seven bearded, vertically challenged men surrounding the bed. She sat up with a start and gasped. One of the men said, 'You see that? Just like a flighty wommon: resting peacefully one minute, up and screaming the next.'

'I agree,' said another. 'She'll disrupt our strong bond of brotherhood and create competition among us for her affections. I say we throw her in the river in a sack full of rocks.'

'I agree we should get rid of her,' said a third, 'but why degrade the ecology? Let's just feed her to a bear or something and let her become part of the food chain?'

'Hear, hear!'

'Sound thinking, brother.'

When Snow White finally regained her senses, she begged, 'Please, please don't kill me. I meant no harm by sleeping on your bed. I thought no one would ever notice.'

'Ah, you see?' said one of the men. 'Female preoccupations are already surfacing. She's complaining that we don't make our beds.'

'Kill her! Kill her!'

'Please, no!' she cried. 'I have travelled so deep into these woods because my mother-of-step, the queen, ordered me to be killed.'

'See that? Internecine female vindictiveness!'

'Don't try and play the victim with *us*, kid!'

'QUIET!' boomed one of the men, who had flaming red hair and a non-human animal skin on his head. Snow White quickly realised that he was their leader and that her fate rested in his hands. 'Explain yourself. What's your name, and why have you really come here?'

'My name is Snow White,' she began, 'and I've already told you: my mother-of-step, the queen, ordered a woodspersun to take me into the forest and kill me, but he took pity and told me to run away into the woods as far as I could.'

'Just like a wommon,' grumbled one of the men under his breath. 'Get a man to do her dirty work.'

The leader held up his hands for silence. He said, 'Well, Snow White, if that's your story, I suppose we'll have to believe you.'

Snow White was beginning to resent her treatment but tried not to let it show. 'And who are you people, anyway?'

'We are known as the Seven Towering Giants,' said the leader. Snow White's suppression of a giggle did not go unnoticed. The leader continued. 'We are towering in *spirit* and so *are giants* among the men of the forest. We used to earn our living by digging in our mines, but we decided that such a rape of the planet was immoral and short-sighted (besides, the bottom fell out of the metals market). So now we are dedicated stewards of the earth and live here in harmony with nature. To make ends meet, we also conduct retreats for men who need to get in touch with their primitive masculine identities.'

'So what does that involve,' asked Snow White, 'aside from drinking milk straight from the carton?'

'Your sarcasm is ill advised,' warned the leader of the Seven Towering Giants. 'My fellow giants want to get rid of your corrupting feminine presence, and I might not be able to stop them, understand? My men, we must speak our hearts openly and honestly. Let us adjourn to the sweat lodge!'

The seven little men scampered out of the front door, whooping and stripping off their clothes. Snow White didn't know what to do while waiting. For fear of stepping on anything that might be scurrying about amid the debris on the floor, she stayed on the bed, although she did manage to make it without ever stepping off.

Snow White heard drumming and shouts, and, soon after, the Seven Towering Giants came back into the cottage. They didn't smell as bad as she thought they would, and thankfully they all wore loincloths.

'Agggh! Look what she's done to my bed! I want her out of here! I want to change my vote!'

'Calm down, brother,' said the leader. 'Don't you see? This is just what we were talking about: contrasts. We can better measure our progress as true men if there is a female around for comparison.'

The men grumbled among themselves about the

wisdom of this decision. But Snow White had had enough. 'I resent being kept around like an object, just a yardstick for your egos and penises!'

'Fair enough,' the leader said. 'You're free to make your way back through the woods. Give our regards to the queen.'

'Well, I suppose I can stay until I work out a new plan,' she said.

'Very well,' said the leader, 'but we have a few ground rules. No dusting. No tidying up. And no rinsing out underwear in the sink.'

'And no peeking in the sweat lodge.'

'And stay away from our drums.'

Meanwhile, back at the castle, the queen rejoiced at the thought that her rival in beauty had been eliminated. She pottered around her boudoir reading *Glamour* and *Elk*, and indulged herself with three whole pieces of chocolate without purging. Later, she confidently strolled up to her magic mirror and asked her same, sad question:

'Mirror, mirror, on the wall,
Who's the fairest one of all?'

The mirror replied,

'Your weight is perfect for your shape and height,
But for sheer OOOOMPH! you can't beat Snow
   White.'

At this news, the queen clenched her fists and screamed at the top of her lungs. For years, her insecurities had been eating away at her until now they turned her into someone who was morally out of the mainstream. With cunning and malice, she began to devise a plan to ensure the non-viability of her daughter-of-step.

A few days later, Snow White, to be sure she didn't touch or rearrange anything, was meditating on the floor in the middle of the cottage. Suddenly there was a knock on the door. Snow White opened the door to find a chronologically gifted wommon with a basket in her hand. By the look of her clothes, she was apparently unfettered by the confines of regular employment.

'Help a wommon of unreliable income, dearie,' she said, 'and buy one of my apples.'

Snow White thought for a moment. In protest against agribusiness conglomerates, she had a persunal rule against buying food from middlepersuns. But her heart went out to the economically marginalised wommon, so she said yes. What Snow White didn't know was that this was really the queen in disguise and that the apple had been chemically and genetically altered so that whoever bit it would sleep for ever.

When Snow White handed over the money for the apple, you would have expected the queen to be gleeful that her plan for revenge was working. Instead, as she looked at Snow White's fine complexion and slim, taut body, she felt alternating waves of envy and self-revulsion. Finally, she burst into tears.

'Why, whatever is the matter?' asked Snow White.

'You're so young and beautiful,' sobbed the disguised queen, 'and I'm horrible to look at and getting worse.'

'You shouldn't say that. After all, beauty comes from inside a persun.'

'I've been telling myself that for years,' said the queen, 'and I still don't believe it. How do you stay in such perfect shape?'

'Well, I meditate, work out in step aerobics three hours a day and eat only half-portions of anything placed in front of me. Would you like me to show you?'

'Oh, yes, yes, please,' said the queen. So they

started out with thirty minutes of simple hatha yoga meditation, then worked out on the step for another hour. As they relaxed afterwards, Snow White cut her apple in half and gave a piece to the queen. Without thinking, the queen bit into it, and both of them fell into a deep sleep.

Later that day, the Seven Towering Giants returned from a retreat in the woods, elaborately decked out in animal skins, feathers and mud. With them was a prince from a nearby kingdom, who had come on this male retreat to find a cure for his impotence (or, as he preferred to call it, his involuntary suspension from phallocentric activity). They were all laughing and back-slapping until they saw the bodies and stopped short.

'What has happened?' asked the prince.

'Apparently our house guest and this other wommon got into some sort of catfight and killed each other,' surmised one giant.

'If they thought that by doing this they could make us slaves to our weaker emotions, they're wrong,' fumed another.

'Well, since we've got to dispose of them, let's practise one of those Viking funerals we've read about.'

'You know,' said the prince, 'this might sound a little sick, but I trust you chaps. I find that younger one attractive. Extremely attractive. Would you fellows mind . . . um . . . waiting outside while I . . .?'

'Stop right there!' said the leader of the giants. 'Those half-eaten apple pieces, that filthy costume – this has all the earmarks of some sort of magic spell. They're not really dead at all.'

'Whew,' sighed the prince, 'that makes me feel better. So could you chaps take a break and let me . . .?'

'Hold it, Prince,' said the leader. 'Does Snow White make you feel like a *man* again?'

'She certainly does. Now, could you chaps—'

'Don't touch her! You'll break the spell.' The leader thought for a minute and said, 'My brothers, I see certain economic possibilities arising from this. If we kept Snow White around here in this state, we could advertise our retreats as impotence therapy.'

The giants nodded in agreement with this idea, but the prince interrupted: 'But what about me? I've already paid for my retreat. Why can't I, um, take the cure?'

'No dice, Prince,' said the leader. 'You can look but don't touch. Otherwise you'll break the spell.

Tell you what, though. You can have the other one if you want.'

'I don't want to sound classist,' said the prince, 'but she's not high enough *calibre* for me.'

'That's pretty big talk from a man shooting blanks,' said one of the giants, and everybody but the prince laughed.

The leader said, 'Come on, brothers, let's lift these two off the floor and decide how we can best display them.' It took three giants for each female, but they managed to get both bodies aloft. As soon as they did, however, the pieces of poisoned apple fell from the mouths of Snow White and the queen, and they awoke from the spell.

'What do you think you're doing? Put us down!' they shouted. The giants were so startled they almost dropped the womyn to the floor.

'That was the most sickening thing I have ever heard!' shouted the queen. 'Offering us around like pieces of property!'

'And *you*,' said Snow White to the prince, 'trying to make it with a girl in a coma! Yuck!'

'Hey, don't blame me,' said the prince. 'It's a medical condition.'

The leader of the giants said, 'Don't start tossing

blame around. You both broke into our property in the first place. I can call the police!'

'Don't try it, Napoleon,' said the queen. 'This forest is property of the crown. *You* are the ones who are trespassing!' This rejoinder caused quite a stir, but not as big a commotion as when the queen warned, 'And another thing. While we were immobile and you all blathered on in your sexist way, I had a persunal awakening. From now on, I am going to dedicate my life to healing the rift between womyn's souls and their bodies. I am going to teach womyn to accept their natural body images and become whole again. Snow White and I are going to build a womyn's spa and conference centre on this very spot, where we can hold retreats, caucuses and ovariums for the sisters of the world.'

There was much shouting and name-calling, but the queen eventually had her way. Before the Seven Towering Giants could be evicted from their home, though, they packed up their sweat lodge and moved deeper into the woods. The prince stayed on at the spa as a cute but harmless tennis pro. And Snow White and the queen became good friends and earned worldwide fame for their contributions to sisterhood. The giants were never heard of again,

save for little muddy footprints that were sometimes found in the morning outside the windows of
the spa's locker room.

Chicken Little

hicken Little lived down a winding country lane surrounded by tall oak trees. (It should be mentioned here that the name 'Little' was a family name, and not a derogatory, size-biased nickname. It was only by sheer coincidence that Chicken Little was also of shorter-than-average height.) One day, Chicken Little was playing in the road when a gust of wind blew through the trees. An acorn was blown loose and hit Chicken Little squarely on the head.

Now, while Chicken Little had a small brain in the physical sense, she did use it to the best of her abilities. So when she screamed, 'The sky is falling, the sky is falling!' her conclusion was not wrong or stupid or silly, only logically under-enhanced.

Chicken Little ran down the road until she came to the house of her neighbour Henny Penny, who was tending her garden. This was a simple task, since she didn't use any insecticide, herbicide or fertiliser, and also permitted the native non-edible varieties of wild-flower (sometimes branded 'weeds') to mingle with her food crops. So, lost amid the foliage, Henny Penny heard Chicken Little's voice long before she saw her.

'The sky is falling! The sky is falling!'

Henny Penny stuck her head out from her garden and said, 'Chicken Little! Why are you carrying on so?'

Chicken Little said, 'I was playing in the road when a huge chunk of the sky fell and landed on my head. See? Here's the bump to prove it.'

'There's just one thing to do,' said Henny Penny.

'What's that?' asked Chicken Little.

'Sue the bastards!' said Henny Penny.

Chicken Little was puzzled. 'Sue for what?'

'Persunal injury, discrimination, intentional infliction of emotional distress, negligent infliction of emotional distress, tortious interference, the tort of outrage – you name it, we'll sue for it.'

'Good gracious!' said Chicken Little. 'What will we get for all that?'

'We can get payment for pain and suffering, compensatory damages, punitive damages, disability and disfigurement, long-term care, mental anguish, impaired earning power, loss of esteem . . .'

'Persun, oh, persun!' said Chicken Little joyfully. 'Who are we going to sue?'

'Well, I don't think the sky per se is recognised as a suable entity by the state,' said Henny Penny.

'I think we should go and find a lawyer and learn who *is* suable,' said Chicken Little, her diminutive brain working overtime.

'That's a good idea. And while we're there, I can ask who to sue for these ridiculously bony legs of mine. They've caused me nothing but anguish and embarrassment all my life, and I should be compensated for all that.'

So they ran further down the road until they came to the house of their neighbour Goosey Loosey. Goosey Loosey was busy teaching her canine animal companion to eat grass so that she could avoid the guilty feelings that came with feeding the dog processed animal carcasses from a can.

'The sky is falling! The sky is falling!'

'Sue the bastards! Sue the bastards!' Goosey Loosey leaned over her fence and said, 'Land sakes! Why are you two carrying on so?'

'I was playing in the road and a piece of sky fell on my head,' explained Chicken Little.

'So we're going to find a lawyer to tell us who we can sue both for her injuries and for my bony legs.'

'Oh good! Can I come and sue someone for my long, gangly neck? You know, nothing really flatters it, so I am convinced there's a conspiracy within the fashion industry against long-necked waterfowl.'

So the three of them ran down the road looking for legal assistance.

'The sky is falling! The sky is falling!'

'Sue the bastards! Sue the bastards!'

'Smash the conspiracy! Smash the conspiracy!'

Further down the road they met Foxy Loxy, who was dressed in a blue suit and carried a briefcase. He held up a paw to halt the entourage.

'And what are you three doing out on this lovely day?' asked Foxy Loxy.

'We're looking for someone to sue!' they shouted in unison.

'What are your grievances? Personal injury? Discrimination? Intentional infliction of emotional distress? Negligent infliction of emotional distress? Tortious interference? The tort of outrage?'

'Oh, yes, yes,' the three said excitedly, 'all that and more!'

'Well, then, you're in luck,' said Foxy Loxy. 'My caseload has just eased up, so I will be able to represent you in any and all lawsuits we can manage to bring.'

The trio cheered and flapped their wings. Chicken Little asked, 'But who are we going to sue?'

Without missing a beat, Foxy Loxy said, 'Who *aren't* we going to sue? Three hapless victims such as yourselves will be able to find more guilty parties than you can shake a writ at. Now, let's all step into my office so we can discuss this further.'

Foxy Loxy walked over to a small black metal door that was in the side of a small hill nearby. 'Step right this way,' he said as he lifted the latch. But the black door wouldn't open. Foxy Loxy tugged on it with one paw, then with both. It still wouldn't budge. He yanked and pulled violently, cursing the door, its mental abilities and its sexual history.

Finally the door swung open, and a huge ball of fire shot out. This was really the door to Foxy Loxy's oven! But unfortunately for him, the ball of fire engulfed his head, burned off every hair and whisker, and left him totally catatonic. Chicken Little, Henny Penny and Goosy Loosey ran away, thankful that they had not been devoured.

However, the family of Foxy Loxy caught up with them. In addition to suing the manufacturer of the oven door on behalf of Foxy Loxy, the family brought a suit against the three above-mentioned barnyard fowl, claiming entrapment, reckless endangerment and fraud. The family sought payment for pain and suffering, compensatory damages, punitive damages, disability and disfigurement, long-term care, mental anguish, impaired earning power, loss of esteem and the loss of a good dinner. The three birds later brought a countersuit, and they've all been battling in court from that day to this.

The Frog Prince

nce there was a young princess who, when she grew tired of beating her head against the male power structure at her castle, would relax by walking into the woods and sitting beside a small pond. There she would amuse herself by tossing her favourite golden ball up and down and pondering the role of the eco-feminist warrior in her era.

One day, while she was dreaming of the Utopia that her queendom could become if womyn were in the positions of power, she dropped the ball, which rolled into the pond. The pond was so deep and murky she couldn't see where it had gone. She didn't cry, of course, but she made a mental note to be more careful next time.

Suddenly she heard a voice say, 'I can get your ball for you, Princess.'

She looked round and saw the head of a frog popping above the surface of the pond. 'No, no,' she said, 'I would never enslave a member of another species to work for my selfish desires.'

The frog said, 'Well, what if we make a deal on a contingency basis? I'll get your ball for you if you do me a favour in return.'

The princess gladly agreed to this most equitable arrangement. The frog dived under the water and soon emerged with the golden ball in his mouth. He spat the ball on the bank and said, 'Now that I've done you a favour, I'd like to explore your views on physical attraction between the species.'

The princess couldn't imagine what the frog was talking about. The frog continued, 'You see, I am not really a frog at all. I'm really a man, but an evil sorcerer has cast a spell on me. While my frog form is no better or worse – only different – than my human form, I would so much like to be among people again. And the only thing that can break this spell is a kiss from a princess.'

The princess thought for a moment about whether

sexual harassment could take place between species, but her heart went out to the frog for his predicament. She bent down and kissed the frog on the forehead. Instantly the frog grew and changed. And there, standing in the water where the frog had been, was a man in a golf shirt and loud plaid trousers – middle-aged, vertically challenged and losing a little bit of hair on top.

The princess was taken aback. 'I'm sorry if this sounds a little classist,' she stammered, 'but ... what I mean to say is ... don't sorcerers usually cast their spells on *princes*?'

'Ordinarily, yes,' he said, 'but this time the target was just an innocent businessman. You see, I'm a real-estate developer, and the sorcerer thought I was cheating him in a property-line dispute. So he invited me out for a round of golf, and just as I was about to tee off, he transformed me. But my time as a frog wasn't wasted, you know. I've got to know every square inch of these woods, and I think it would be ideal for an office/property share/resort complex. The location's great and the numbers add up perfectly! The bank wouldn't lend any money to a frog, but now that I'm in human form again, they'll be eating out of my hand. Oh, will that be sweet! And let me tell you, this is going to be a big project! Just drain the pond, cut down about 80 per cent of the trees, get easements for—'

The frog developer was cut short when the princess shoved her golden ball back into his mouth. She then pushed him back underwater and held him there until he stopped thrashing. As she walked back to the castle, she marvelled at the number of good deeds that a persun could do in just one morning. And while someone might have noticed that the frog was gone, no one ever missed the real-estate developer.

Jack and the Beanstalk

nce upon a time, on a little farm, there lived a boy named Jack. He lived on the farm with his mother, and they were very excluded from the normal circles of economic activity. This cruel reality kept them in straits of direness, until one day Jack's mother told him to take the family cow into town and sell it for as much as he could.

Never mind the thousands of gallons of milk they had stolen from her! Never mind the hours of pleasure their bovine animal companion had provided! And forget about the manure they had appropriated for their garden! She was now just another piece of property to them. Jack, who didn't realise that non-human animals have as many rights as human animals – perhaps even more – did as his mother asked.

On his way to town, Jack met an old magic vegetarian, who warned Jack of the dangers of eating beef and dairy products.

'Oh, I'm not going to eat this cow,' said Jack. 'I'm going to take her into town and sell her.'

'But by doing that, you'll just perpetuate the cultural mythos of beef, ignoring the negative impact of the cattle industry on our ecology and the health and social problems that arise from meat consumption. But you look too simple to be able to make these connections, my boy. I'll tell you what I'll do: I'll offer to trade your cow for these three magic beans, which have as much protein as that entire cow but none of the fat or sodium.'

Jack made the swap gladly and took the beans home to his mother. When he told her about the deal he had made, she grew very upset. She used to think her son was merely a conceptual rather than a linear thinker, but now she was sure that he was downright differently abled. She grabbed the three magic beans and threw them out of the window in disgust. Later that day, she attended her first support-group meeting with Mothers of Storybook Children.

The next morning, Jack stuck his head out of the window to see if the sun had risen in the east again (he was beginning to see a pattern in this). But outside the window, the beans had grown into a huge stalk that reached through the clouds. Because he no longer had a cow to milk in the morning, Jack climbed the beanstalk into the sky.

At the top, above the clouds, he found a huge castle. It was not only big, but it was built to larger-than-average scale, as if it were the home of someone who just happened to be a giant. Jack entered the castle and heard beautiful music wafting through the air. He followed this sound until he found its source: a golden harp that played music without being touched. Next to this self-actualised harp was a hen sitting on a pile of golden eggs.

Now, the prospect of easy wealth and mindless entertainment appealed to Jack's bourgeois sensibilities, so he picked up both the harp and the hen and started to run for the front door. Then he heard thundering footsteps and a booming voice that said, 'FEE, FIE, FOE, FUM, I smell the blood of an English persun! I'd like to learn about his culture and views on life! And share my own perspectives in an open and generous way!'

Unfortunately, Jack was too crazed with greed to accept the giant's offer of a cultural interchange. *It's only a trick*, thought Jack. *Besides, what's a giant doing with such fine, delicate things? He must have stolen them from somewhere else, so I have every right to take them.* His frantic justifications – remarkable for someone with his overtaxed mental resources – revealed a terrible callousness to the giant's persunal rights. Jack apparently was a complete sizeist, who thought that all giants were clumsy, knowledge-impaired and exploitable.

When the giant saw Jack with the magic harp and the hen, he asked, 'Why are you taking what belongs to me?'

Jack knew he couldn't outrun the giant, so he had to think fast. He blurted out, 'I'm not taking them, my friend. I am merely placing them in my stewardship so that they can be properly managed and brought to their fullest potential. Pardon my bluntness, but you giants are too simple in the head and don't know how to manage your resources properly. I'm just looking after your interests. You'll thank me for this later.'

Jack held his breath to see if the bluff would save his skin. The giant sighed heavily and said, 'Yes, you are right. We giants do use our resources foolishly. Why, we can't even discover a new beanstalk without getting so excited and picking away at it so much that we pull the poor thing right out of the ground!'

Jack's heart sank. He turned and looked out of the front door of the castle. Sure enough, the giant had destroyed his beanstalk. Jack grew frightened and cried, 'Now I'm trapped here in the clouds with you for ever!'

The giant said, 'Don't worry, my little friend. We are strict vegetarians up here, and there are always plenty of beans to eat. And besides, you won't be alone. Thirteen other men of your size have already climbed up beanstalks to visit us and stayed.'

So Jack resigned himself to his fate as a member of the giant's cloud commune. He didn't miss his mother or their farm much, because up in the sky there was less work to do and more than enough to eat. And he gradually learned not to judge people based on their size ever again, except for those shorter than he.

The Pied Piper of Hamelin

he picturesque little town of Hamelin had everything a community could wish for – non-polluting industries, effective public transport and a well balanced ethno-religious diversity. In fact, the town council had managed to legislate or intimidate away every element that could keep the citizens from living a good and sensitive life. Every element, that is, except the caravan site.

The caravan site on the edge of Hamelin was a civic embarrassment. Not only was it a terrible eyesore, with its rusted pick-up vans and rubbish heaps in every backyard. Within it dwelled some of the most unregenerate and irredeemable people you could ever imagine – murderers of non-domestic animals, former clients of the correctional system and cross-country bikers. With their plastic daisy windmills, loud music and drunken weekend brawls, they sent a shudder through every respectable persun in town.

One day, after a particularly riotous road rally through the caravan site, the town council had a meeting. After heated debate, they decided that somehow they had to eradicate the caravan site. But they were at a loss to know how to do it without ignoring or infringing upon the rights of the people who lived there. Finally, after even more oratory, they decided to let that be someone else's worry, since they were already so burdened with more important concerns, such as declining property values. So the councillors decided to advertise for someone to solve their problem.

Soon after the advertisement was sent out, a man appeared in town. He was very vertically gifted and of lower than average weight for his size. His clothes were worn in combinations never before seen or imagined, and his mannerisms and high-pitched voice were certainly unique. Although he looked as if he came from some world other than (but certainly not unequal to) our own, he gained the trust of the desperate town councillors.

'I will be able to rid your town of the caravan site dwellers,' said the man of enhanced strangeness, 'but you must promise to pay me a hundred pieces of gold.'

The town councillors wanted this whole unpleasant business finished as soon as possible, so they readily assented. The sooner the caravan site was eliminated, the sooner they could all revert to their open-minded, progressive selves.

So the man of enhanced strangeness got down to work. He reached into his tattered knapsack and pulled out a sophisticated, compact recording machine. The people around him looked on with interest as he inserted a few tapes, set some knobs and checked the sound levels. Then he began mumbling into the built-in microphone. No one could hear exactly what he was saying, but the man seemed to be lacking in coherence. Abruptly, he stopped mumbling, stood up and told the town councillors that he needed a van with a public-address system.

The authorities scrambled after this strange request. They managed to find such a van at the Department of Public Biodiversity and handed over the keys to the man of enhanced strangeness. He climbed in and drove off, popping the cassette he had made into the sound system. Everyone followed the van as it headed towards the caravan site.

Soon music began to emerge from the slowly moving van – generally pop music but also occasional classics like 'The Ballad of the Green Berets' and 'Ghost Riders in the Sky'. The town councillors were puzzled by this, until they noticed people emerging from their caravans, tool sheds and taverns. The people had a certain glassy expression and talked to themselves as they stumbled along.

'I'm going to find a job,' said one. 'I hear the funfair is taking people on.'

'I think I'll join the professional stock-car racing circuit,' said another.

'Do you think I could make a living by signing up for medical experiments?' asked a third.

The denizens of the caravan site followed the van as it drove slowly towards the edge of town. Soon both they and it disappeared over the horizon, and the town councillors raised a cheer.

About an hour later the van returned, minus its entourage. 'I led them all to the main road,' said the man of enhanced strangeness as he alighted from the van. 'They're out thumbing lifts to anywhere but Hamelin. Now the caravan site is free for you to use in whatever way you want.'

'Marvellous!' said one of the authorities, who was serving as a spokespersun. 'Now that they're gone, we can commence with our plans for a Third World Refugee Reorientation Centre. Thank you, thank you.'

'Now, if you will kindly pay me the hundred pieces of gold you promised, I'll be on my way.'

'Well, er ... Hamelin is striving to establish an economy that is based on human capital and not the mere exploitation of physical resources. And so, to this end, we'd like to offer you this coupon book, which entitles you to such services in Hamelin as free massages and seminars on releasing your inner child.'

The man of enhanced strangeness squinted his eyes. 'You promised me a hundred pieces of gold,' he said, growing visibly angry. 'Now pay up or suffer the consequences.'

'If you wish to abandon your responsibility for making the world a more equitable place,' clucked the spokespersun, 'so be it. We will have to give you the official Hamelin IOU, which can be redeemed for a significant portion of its face value at many of the post offices and off-licences in the surrounding towns.'

The man of enhanced strangeness paused, then chuckled eerily and climbed back in the van. Before anyone could stop him, he began to drive through all the residential areas of Hamelin. As he went, the van played a weird, high-pitched music that no one could recognise. Soon, the children of Hamelin emerged from their houses and streamed from their playgrounds. With glazed looks, they milled about in the streets. The town councillors could hear the children talking earnestly to each other.

'Free markets are the only sure way to give people the persunal incentive to build a better society,' said one child.

'We must respect the rights of citizens to pre-serve the ethnic purity of their neighbourhoods,' said another.

'Our only obligation as a society is to make sure everyone has a level playing field,' said a third.

As their children began to form tax protest groups and shooting clubs, the town councillors sadly real-ised that all their years of careful social planning would soon come to nothing. The next day, they found the public-address van on the outskirts of town, but there was no sign of the mysterious man whom they had tried to swindle.

The Duckling That Was Judged on its Persunal Merits and not on its Physical Appearance

Now I'd like to tell you the story of the duckling that was judged on its persunal merits and not on its physical appearance. A very happy little tale that would be.

Such a story would be *completely* make-believe, of course. The world would never be so kind-hearted or fair. To anthropomorphise barnyard ducks with these generous traits would be ridiculous, especially if they are meant to represent people in a fable like this one.

So instead I will tell you a story of a poor egg, displaced by who knows what misfortune, that fell through the barnyard social safety net (not literally, for that would result in a very short story) and found itself in the nest of a Mama Duck. This Mama Duck was single and proud of it, and she was happy to take on this extra responsibility. Among all its nestmates, there was no way to tell that this egg was special. Of course, each egg was special in its own way, but this one was *especially* special. When all the ducklings hatched, it was clear that one of them was so very special that her face could stop a sundial.

'Oh my' said Mama Duck, running through a mental list of all the male ducks she'd known in the past few months. What had gone on during that weekend in Copenhagen? It was awfully dark, but had she really been that stoned?

But appearances mattered not at all to the differently pretty duckling. She swam like her brothers and sisters. She ate weeds like her brothers and sisters. She tormented mentally challenged hunters with slapstick and practical jokes like her brothers and sisters.

Still, the Mama Duck could not be comforted. She had big plans for her ducklings: enrolment in the best private schools, dance and gymnastics lessons, tennis camp, summer internships in the capital. That was all endangered now, because of the lookist biases of both society and herself.

Maybe we could test the ugly one, she said to herself, revealing who was truly the ugly one. *If we found she had a learning disability – a small manageable one, of course, not a big one – a school would have to give her accommodations and she'd get better grades. Heaven knows the little thing needs a web up!*

Deep down, Mama Duck was quite the Yuddie. Everything had to be just so for her brood to move up in the world. The unfulfilled dreams for her own life caused her to put way too much pressure on her offspring. In one of her biggest obsessions, she entered her ducklings in junior beauty pageants for the barnyard. It was a sad sight indeed to watch the ducklings try and tap-dance with gobs of eye make-up and glitter and mousse in their feathers.

In response, the cosmetically challenged duckling organised her own competitions for the youngsters around. They competed in science fairs and photography contests, organised blood drives and held soccer tournaments in which no one kept score and everyone was a winner.

As she grew older, the alternatively attractive duckling became even more self-confident. She had an inner strength that allowed her to keep her mother's problems from damaging her own self-esteem.

Sure, the duckling had her phases. She went punk for a while, then Goth, and did some experimentation with another she-duck in college. But through it all, she was very happy to be who she was, and thumbed her beak at the hang-ups of the rest of the barnyard.

Some animals thought she had a little too much attitude. Whispers began behind her back: 'That ugly duckling is just overcompensating because she can't get a date. Even the loons won't go out with her, and they'd do it with a decoy.'

To fight these shallow notions, the duckling began to speak out about animals accepting their own bodies. She was a charismatic speaker, and her lisp made her even more endearing. 'We are all beautiful inside,' she would tell everyone. 'Who cares that some of us are graceful and others aren't? We can accomplish great things when we stop worrying about what we all look like.'

Soon, and despite her good intentions, she began to be idolised by the animals that are rarely perceived as cute and cuddly. The armadillos followed her around with stars in their eyes, and the warthogs hung on her every word (as you can tell, this was a very inclusive barnyard).

As time went on, however, the other animals noticed a change in the duckling. And the duckling began to notice a change in their attitudes towards her. The animals who had been her friends seemed to treat her coldly and eventually drifted away. At the same time, the animals she previously had disagreed with (including her mother) began to accept her more readily.

By accident, she caught a glimpse of herself in the calm water of the pond. She didn't recognise what was looking back. Instead of motley earthtone feathers, she was now covered in smooth white down. Instead of a uniquely gangly neck, she now beheld a long, slender one.

She was no longer a duckling with an individual style that went counter to the dominant beauty paradigm. She was now a graceful and elegant swan!

'Bwaahhh!' she cried. 'Look at me! What's happened?'

'Aww,' smiled the other animals, 'isn't she just the *cutest* when she cries?'

'Don't condescend to me!' she shouted.

'My my,' said everyone, 'that's a mighty big word for such a pretty little thing! And that lisp! Adorable!'

The former duckling left them and went to find

her adoring fans. She begged them, 'Don't hate me because I'm beautiful!'

The warthog and the armadillo frowned and said, 'We don't. We hate you because you're a swan.'

And so, because of the lookist prejudices of barnyard society, the former duckling had an impossible time getting anyone to take her seriously again. Even on such life-and-death issues as protesting against foie gras (RIP Mama Duck), no one listened to a word she said. The sad little thing spent the rest of her days floating around with the other swans, who could talk about nothing else but fashion, spa visits and reality TV shows.

Pinocchio

Chapter 1

Many years ago, in a picturesque village lived a carpenter named Geppetto. His small-footprint house/workspace was neat and clean and energy efficient. Throughout his life, Geppetto had been single, never 'taking' a wife, a partner, a mistress or a regular sexual surrogate of any kind. Geppetto used to tell people, 'I'm alone, but not lonely,' and divided his leisure hours between positive journaling and goat yoga.

In time, however, Geppetto felt the need to pass his life knowledge on to someone else. Since the official agencies frowned upon on an economically marginalised, seventy-five-year-old hermit adopting a child, Geppetto decided to meet his need for company his own way. He chose a log of seasoned ash (no tropical hardwoods in *his* shop). He picked up his tools and began to chisel away. Soon, in a wonderful display of primitive craftspersunship, Geppetto finished his indigenous artisanal companion.

'That's a good day's work,' Geppetto said. 'Tomorrow I will teach him all I know about carpentry, life, love and self-actualisation. And I will call him Pinocchio.' He then lit a candle, turned down the thermostat and toddled off to bed.

Just as Geppetto's head hit his ergonomically designed pillow, a quivering light appeared in his workshop and fluttered in the air. From that mystickal light emerged a young wommon in a flowing blue gown that glittered like an unpolluted sea at midday. Using her delicate wings, she glided over to the workbench where the puppet sat and touched him with her powerful wand, subverting its sad, phallic imagery for her own vivifying purposes. Slowly, the puppet stirred and moved his head and blinked his eyes in wonder.

'Hello,' said the blue wommon to the persun of log.

'Wh-where am I?' the puppet asked. 'Wh-who are you? Wow, are you a fairy?'

She sighed and answered, 'I am an *individual*

who just happens to *be* a fairy. I have more facets to my persunality than can be adequately described by some limiting label. Don't pigeonhole me with your preconceptions about what a fairy should and should not be.'

'G-gosh, I'm real sorry,' he said.

'And don't even *think* of asking me to smile more.'

'Oh, never, never!' What a world of accelerated unusualness he was now in!

The magickal wommon's demeanour softened a bit. 'This is a very lucky day for you, Pinocchio.'

'Hey, hold on a minute,' he said. 'Why do you call me that?'

'Because that is your name.'

'But no one consulted *me*. That's not fair. Don't I and I alone have the right to name myself?'

'Of course you do,' agreed the aethereal visitor. 'I apologise. What name can you think of that fully describes your position in the world and your philosophy of life, and is free of the barbaric exploitation and bigoted assumptions of the inherited cultural paradigm?'

'Um . . . what?'

She fluttered a few seconds. 'Just relax, and a name will come to you.'

The puppet frowned in thought, then declared, 'I choose to call myself . . . Rumpelstiltskin!'

Her smile faltered. 'It's been done.'

'Howdy Doody?'

'Ummm . . .'

'Well,' said the eager little puppet, 'how about . . . Pinocchio?'

'A wise and responsible choice for a puppet of such tender years,' said the reality-queer persun. 'As I was saying, this is a very lucky day for you. You have been granted life! And if you live a correct and progressive one, avoid red meat and work hard to become fully evolved (though not at the expense of others), you will turn into a real boy!'

All this was too much for Pinocchio to grasp. So many possibilities, so many conditions, so many strings attached! Finally he said, 'Wait a second. You're assuming that becoming a hummon is the be-all and end-all of everything. If I were to go hominid, I'd be turning my back on my puppetal origins! I'm not sure that's what I want at all.'

'You are right. I imposed my anthropocentric biases on to you. Life is long, Pinocchio, and you will go through many changes. When the time—'

'And what's with the gender bias? I was made

with male parts – so what? Everyone knows there's a huge difference between a physical body and gender identity. Society's toxic messages of masculinity won't—'

'Listen! You're not my only appointment tonight. This is a side gig. When the time is right, I will appear to you again, and we can discuss your metamorphosal options. Until then, consider all viewpoints, practise self-care and stay hydrated. There is much to learn, and just as much (if not more) to unlearn. As we say around the fairy ring, "Now that you been woke, you gotta stay woke."'

With that, the sorcerex disappeared just as she had arrived, and left Pinocchio alone to contemplate his new opportunities.

Chapter 2

Geppetto awoke to find that his nondenominational prayers had been answered. The puppet he had crafted was now alive! The woodcarver danced around and around for joy with his new pal. Then Geppetto explained to the timbered individual it was time for him to go to school.

Pinocchio, of course, objected. He protested that all he would learn would be survivor-biased propaganda, the conformist pressures of mob thinking and the self-serving deceptions of dead white men. But Geppetto insisted. He put a few coins in Pinocchio's hand and sent him off.

On the street, Pinocchio muttered about the injustice of it all: 'Why should I have to go to school, just because I happen to be alive? I didn't ask to be animated.'

As he turned a corner, he came face to face with two strangers: a fox and a cat.

'Whatever is the matter, my young friend?' asked the fox.

'My father is making me go to school against my will. Almost threatened me with a shellacking.'

'Who needs to go to school,' the cat said, 'especially in the prime of youth?'

'Not me,' Pinocchio said. 'It will impede my individuality and warp my persunal expression.'

'Aha! I knew it,' the fox said in a syrupy voice. 'If persunal expression is your paramount concern, take our advice: your sole destination should and must be . . . the theatre! I've known and helped a number of young thespians in my day. You have marvellous potential. Your star quality shines forth like a beacon.'

'Sounds pretty narcissistic to me,' the puppet sneered.

'Not at all! You should come with us to meet someone who will know exactly how to polish your ingrained skills, a facilitator you can trust completely.'

And so they walked together, discussing the veracity of live performance, the social imperative of non-traditional casting and whether improv was inescapably misogynist. Around the corner, over the tracks, down an alley, through the transit authority carriage depot and up a treacherous flight of stairs, they came to a rough door, on which were hand-written the words, 'The Space, LLC'. Inside, the fox introduced Pinocchio to Deward X. Cassel-Dworkin, the founder and artistic director there.

'I'm so very *excited* to meet you, Pinocchio,' he purred. 'Mmmm, I can tell already you'd fit in *perfectly* with our "family" here. *Speaking* of family, do you have any wealthy relatives who would be interested in *underwriting* the efforts of creative explorers such as *we*?'

Pinocchio sadly could only contribute the coins

his father had given him to buy books and a hot lunch. Cassel-Dworkin assured him that of course art didn't take its inspiration from money, and enrolled him in the training centre right away. For the privilege of such tutelage, the puppet handed over all his cash (while the fox and cat took a hefty agent's cut). And with that, Pinocchio rejected Geppetto's conformist agenda and moved into The Space, LLC.

Before long, Pinocchio could feel himself growing as a performer. He enjoyed the primal-scream exercises, exploring the pain of separation from his original log. He also loved hanging out with his fellow actors, nursing coffee in diners, getting piercings and observing life.

The persuns of The Space, LLC did a lot of street theatre to bring their art to the people and save money on space rental. Times were not always lean: enough grants came through to let the troupe mount some important stagings, including a severely Brechtian interpretation of *Bye Bye Birdie*.

But in time Pinocchio's star trajectory began to wane. Despite Cassel-Dworkin's promises about 'non-traditional casting', Pinocchio repeatedly found himself playing coat racks and endtables. He was promised a lead role in *The Cherry Orchard*, but when he learned of the violence the role required, the fledgling wooden thespian baulked.

'How can I express myself in this dual-visaged environment? Compromise and tokenism in every direction. I won't hang around to see what they'll use me for in *The Master Builder*.'

So, on a Monday, when everyone else was out auditioning for sitcoms and industrial shows, Pinocchio sneaked out of The Space, LLC, and continued his quest in search of his true self. He took his headshot postcards with him, though, just in case.

Chapter 3

Pinocchio had pulled back the flimsy veneer of the self-indulgent, boojie theatre world and exposed the rot underneath. But the questions remained: Where would he go? What should he do? Where could a failed, unskilled actor earn a living (except in politics, of course)? All the uncertainty left a knot in his stomach.

As he pondered his future, the persun of log ambled down a road winding through the forest.

The arboreal ecosystem was varied, healthy and sustainable, and it re-centred him nicely. A few of the trees even looked familiar, through he couldn't place the phloem.

A sharp pain in his side made Pinocchio cry out. He reached over and found a wriggly gnawing insect trying to burrow inside him. He held the hitchhiker up for a closer look.

The bug wriggled his legs and said cheerfully, 'Always insist on locally grown food!'

Pinocchio shook him roughly. 'Well, why did it have to be me?'

He was about to turn this tiny parasite into paste, when a blinding flash of light left him visually nonfunctioning. The blue individual skilled in eldritch arts appeared and exclaimed, 'Pinocchio! What are you doing?'

'This cricket is chewing its way inside me!'

'No, no, no,' she corrected, 'that's *not* a cricket!'

'It's not? It sure looks like—'

'No, it most certainly is *not*, and remind me later to instruct you about copyrighted characters and overly litigious entertainment conglomerates.'

The bug piped up, 'The man who represents himself in court has a fool for a client! Ha ha!'

'Arggh!' Pinocchio moaned. 'These annoying sayings! Is this what they mean by a '"microaggression"?'

'I have invited this adorable insect along to be your conscience. It's a safeguard for your future puppetal growth.'

Pinocchio did not like this new development one bit. Why did she think he needed a conscience? Most other persuns got along fine without one.

The bug said, 'We only have one life in which to live our best, but one life should be enough,' and jumped on to Pinocchio and started boring into his trunk again.

'Ow!' said the puppet. 'Stop it! You're being an invasive species!'

With that, an amazing thing happened: the nose on Pinocchio's face doubled in length!

'And now comes safeguard number two,' the blue mystickal wommon said. 'Whenever you lash back with comments that are hateful or exclusionary, your poor little nose will grow.'

The puppet fumed, 'That's a no-good . . .'

'Wait, I'm not finished. Your nose will also grow if you: quote an unreliable news source; use information you know to be untruthful, misleading or only quoted in part; use abusive, profane or discriminatory language; appropriate a culture not your own in a sketch, song, performance or other work, artistic or academic; or create a hostile work or play environment through language, deed or signage.'

'Who's to say what's true or not, anyway?' Pinocchio asked, and his nose immediately grew again.

'And especially if you say ignorant things like that.'

'And for that, you make my nose grow?' Pinocchio sniffed, touching his new wooden protuberance gingerly. 'Pretty lookist, I think! What did I say that was so wrong?'

'Your comment about the insect was unkind, defamatory and speciesist. It didn't consider its own situation. It might have arrived here because of climate change, in which case it would be a displaced, climate-refugee bug. It's a worthwhile species that just happens to be invasive.'

'A moment of silence in a moment of anger,' the bug chuckled from inside Pinocchio, 'will save a hundred moments of regret. Yes sir!'

'Does it have to be so corny?' the puppet asked. 'It's a living, breathing, *biting* Hallmark card.' And with that comment, his nose grew again.

'Better keep those judgements in check,' the sayer

of sooth said, 'unless you'd like a nose that needs training wheels.'

Pinocchio thought about his options for a minute. The sooner he simply did as she asked, the sooner this overbearing sensitivity trainer would leave him alone. 'If anyone misconstrued my statements and was offended,' he said, in a classic dodge, 'I offer an apology.' And the blue wommon, not well versed in public relations or double-speak, took Pinocchio at his word. A flock of birds flew on to his nasal extremity, and pecked and pecked until it was its original size again.

'There,' said the persun of enhanced aethereality, 'all back to how it was. Your conscience will help guide you, Pinocchio. Behave yourself, embrace the truth, and you will be rewarded.'

Pinocchio smiled and nodded, but didn't say anything. Though her endorsement of the status quo sent shivers down his rings, he decided it was best to feign agreement. He could make the bug's death look like an accident after she was gone.

Chapter 4

Pinocchio and his chitinous conscience (still unnamed, for reasons explained in the previous chapter, and definitely not wearing a little top hat, morning coat or spats) continued down the road. The insect still spouted bromides with the zeal of great epiphanies.

'Every end is a new beginning!'

'This is life, not a dress rehearsal!'

'Sometimes "home" is another persun!'

The bug's clichés were starting to grate on Pinocchio even worse than its rasping mandibles, and he grew more set on getting rid of the bug, regardless of the ecological impact. Like many a literary hero/shero/theyro, Pinocchio was determined to discover his destiny on his own, without help from anyone. He had absorbed, even at this young age, the toxic masculine ideas of individual accomplishment and emotional isolation. If he ever did become a real boy, there was most certainly a heart attack in his future.

As he turned a bend in the road, Pinocchio heard the murmur of voices. Soon, he began to see people, a few to start, then more and more. The throng grew, and in time it covered an open grassy plain, with everyone chanting, shouting and raising fists. Pinocchio roamed among the many passionate groups and learned what ideas they were shouting about. He met a group carrying a black flag (which of course made the bug nervous). 'We're anarchists,' they told him. 'We want to smash all oppressive social structures, and let persunkind's natural goodness emerge from the ashes. The *best* system is *no* system! Come to our meeting later.'

'Gosh,' Pinocchio said. 'Where will you be holding your meeting?'

'We haven't agreed on that yet – haven't for thirty-five years – and we're *proud* of it!'

The woke puppet found himself among marchers of all kinds: pro-this, anti-that, always loud and enthusiastic. The slogans of each new group resonated so strongly with him that he eagerly agreed to march with all of them. He found everyone fascinating (except for the insensitive lout who invited him to attend the Burning Man festival).

At the edge of the clearing was a ravine, with a rushing river a few hundred feet below. Pinocchio noticed groups on the opposite side waving their own flags and signs, and yelling nasty things to the people on his side.

'Who are they?' he asked no one in particular.

'Evil! Stupid! Burn them! Destroy them!' came the answer from both sides of the chasm. And that was answer enough for everybody.

One group Pinocchio met was trying to save the planet by eliminating hamburger consumption (named WIMPY – World Is Meat-Poisoned, Yo!). In the group was a young wommon named Kasha. She was a wyld wommon, beautiful and free, and the growth she inspired in the persun of wood was obvious. He admired her knowledge and passion. He also wanted someone who could help guide him through this chaotic world without blinding him with a blue flash every time she showed up.

So after a WIMPY meeting, in which they planned to blow up a few franchises of a globe-strangling fast-food chain, Pinocchio screwed down his courage and said, 'If I may say so, Kasha, I like you.'

'You have my permission,' Kasha said. 'I like you too, Pinocchio. You have an old soul.'

'Oh, I wouldn't say that,' he said, embarrassed by the feeling of his young sap rising.

The bug chimed in, 'Don't put the key to your happiness in someone else's pocket,' but had burrowed in too deep to be heard.

'You're very rooted.' Kasha smiled.

Pinocchio responded, 'There's no doubt in my mind, hamburgers are the thing that's going to destroy the earth!'

While his statement wasn't surprising, the reaction was, as his nose doubled in length!

'Aggh!' Kasha screamed. 'What's going on?'

Pinocchio stammered, 'It . . . it's an allergic reaction to patchouli.'

With that alternative fact, his nose doubled in length again.

'What are you doing? You pig!'

'Let me help you understand. There was this blue fairy, see—'

'Don't you *dare* puppet-splain to me! I know sexual harassment when I see it! I've been violated!'

Kasha picked up a large stick and began to chase Pinocchio. Others who saw his growing schnoz were shocked and yelled at him too. As he ran to escape, many startled people in the crowd were lucky his protruding proboscis didn't spear them.

Pinocchio was running from the angry Kasha so desperately that he didn't see where he was going and fell into the ravine. He tumbled over and over, then splashed in the river and was swept away.

While Kasha went to seek counseling about the incident, others on her side of the ravine erected a safety fence along the edge. Those on the far side, meanwhile, hooted and jeered and shot off guns and fireworks, occasionally falling over the edge themselves, rejoicing in their liberty to do so.

Chapter 5

The river carried Pinocchio mile after mile. The current, propelled by runoff from deforestation, sent him through several river ecosystems and out to the open sea. In the cold water, his nose, like so many things do, shrank to a tiny size. Though weathered and worn, the intrepid puppet looked forward to embarking on a new adventure.

The bug stuck its head out and smiled. 'You can't stop the waves, but you can learn to surf!' At which point, to Pinocchio's relief, a hungry salmon swam up and ate it.

This respite gave Pinocchio a chance to reflect on his life so far. The seagulls whirling overhead and the gentle waves helped him confront his feelings unvarnished. He thought of Geppetto, the individual who happened to be a fairy, the fox and cat, Deward X. Cassel-Dworkin, the unforgettable Kasha. While he had affection for them all, they had all tried to make him conform to those rigid social expectations of what a stringless marionette should be. He yearned to explore the wide spectrum of mannequinism, to break out of the little wooden box people put him in, to splinter the stifling puppet paradigm . . .

His reverie was interrupted by a large whale, as it breached the surface with a mighty splash. In an instant, it had caught Pinocchio in its baleen and dragged him into the brine-fortified deep! And when it resurfaced and opened its mouth, who should Pinocchio see next to him but his father, Geppetto!

'Father! What are you doing here?'

Geppetto's head lolled around, his adventure with the magnificent sea creature providing negative benefits. 'What . . . who's there?'

'It's me, Pinocchio!'

'Sorry,' he tried to speak as he spat out seawater, 'the name's not familiar . . .'

'Not familiar? I left for school just three days ago.'

'Well, you know . . . busy life . . .'

The whale submerged at that point and stayed under for quite some time. When it emerged again, both man and mannequin gasped for air.

'I'd heard krill . . . was a new superfood,' Geppetto choked, 'but you can have it . . .'

'*Now* do you recognise me?'

Geppetto sighed and said, 'Oh, who cares what an old man thinks anyway?'

'Enough with the passive-aggressiveness! Own your emotions!'

Just then, the magickal azure individual appeared and hovered next to them. She wore a disappointed look. 'Is this how you have your fun now, Pinocchio, joy-riding in the mouth of an innocent whale? You think nature is here just for your amusement?'

Pinocchio would have defended himself, had the whale not dived again in its hunt for food. When it resurfaced, she continued, 'And you, Geppetto, a fine example for a father figure to give. What will you be teaching him next? Dynamite fishing?'

'Stop your shaming!' Pinocchio said, coughing seawater. 'It's bad enough that you swoop in to solve things like a know-it-all. You don't have to hammer it home!'

'Do you think I like being your *dea ex machina*?'

she asked, pointing her wand in his face. 'It's repetitive and thankless and extremely stereotypical.'

'Then why are you bothering us?'

'I told you before: it's a side hustle. I'm also an adjunct professor of medieval studies and folklore, but that doesn't pay diddly and I'm up to my wingtips in student debt. Magic pays OK, but I want tenure.'

'Elitist,' the puppet muttered.

'Now, since I have an extension class to teach tonight, let's get this over with. Let me talk to the whale; I'm sure it's as annoyed by this whole situation as I am.'

So the reality-queer persun flew over to the side of the whale's head, and clicked and squeaked a few syllables into its ear hole. In an instant, the cetaceous individual turned and headed for the undeveloped shoreline in the distance.

Chapter 6

On an isolated beach, the right (though not more deserving) whale did the right (for our story) thing. Avoiding the nesting migration of a herd of sea turtles, the whale swam to a safe distance from the shore and blew the puppet and the puppet-maker on to the beach like a couple of cherry pits. They spluttered and coughed, thanked the whale for its thoughtfulness, and plopped down on the sand exhausted.

'I'll admit, it's good to see you, Pinocchio,' Geppetto finally said. 'I didn't know what to do with myself after you disappeared. Just a lonely codependent old man...'

'I've missed you too, Father, despite your guilt trips.'

'... just the persun who carved you into this world, is all.'

Again, a blue flash exploded in front of them. 'Yet I was the one,' said the sorcerex, 'who gave him life.'

'And who was the absentee parent, flying away all the time?' Geppetto countered.

'Dad! Mum! Stop fighting!'

The magickal plot-mover smiled. 'You are right, wise Pinocchio. This should be a happy reunion. The family is back together!'

Geppetto let out a long sigh. 'Yes, well, this *family* thing is a losing proposition for me, I'm afraid. Too much investment, not enough return. I'm not made for it.'

Pinocchio's chin dropped on its hinge. 'What do you mean?' he gulped.

'I mean, we pay so much lip service to the concept of a "happy family" that we inevitably become dissatisfied. No one can live up to the ideal. Besides, I'm not ready to be a father.'

'Not ready? You're seventy-five!'

'But I *am* ready to monetise this. Lots of people are too busy to pay attention to their actual family, but I could carve them one, to their exact specifications! Big, small, all conforming to conventional beauty standards. Be surrounded by the family you want, whenever you want! Already happening in Japan, I hear. So, goodbye, good luck! You've had your chance to roam for fame and fortune. Now it's my turn.'

Geppetto got up and walked down the beach, just another man abdicating his responsibilities. Pinocchio felt like crying.

'How disappointing,' sighed the individual who happened to be a fairy. 'If only he were made of wood . . .'

Pinocchio said, 'Who'd have thought so much

commercial exploitation was in my roots? Lucky for me my natural parents weren't hummon.'

'Pinocchio,' she said, 'I'm not your birth mother, or your birth tree, but I'm very proud of you nonetheless. You have taken your quest for persunal evolution seriously, if somewhat erratically. Your inclusive heart and your social conscience both grew, along with your nose.'

'It's the journey, not the destination, that matters,' Pinocchio mused, wincing at the idea that the bug's stale adages had had an effect on him.

'Bravo, well said. Now, because of your honesty and hard work, I will reward you by turning you into a real, live—'

'If you're going to say "boy", then stop right there. I told you in the beginning not to assume that I wanted to become a hummon, especially not a male. One thing I've learned in my travels is I don't want to join a group so destructive and hateful to the planet and other species, as well as themselves.'

The persun of wizardly skills was stunned and embarrassed for a moment. 'Yes, you did tell me that. Well, I'm sort of at a loss then. Most animate and inanimate beings I meet in my line of work want to become hummon – and usually rich, handsome and happy for the rest of their lives.'

'Oh, how shallow,' Pinocchio scoffed. 'I really pity such creatures, clamouring to be something they're not. My adventures have taught me to accept myself, knots and all. In my quest, I've found so much of my nurturing, fertile side that I know exactly what I would like to become!'

'And what is that, my dearest Pinocchio?'

Pinocchio thrust out his chest and said proudly, 'A pile of mulch!'

And so ends our story of the little ligneous homunculus. The persun of fairyhood granted Pinocchio's wish and transformed him into a rich, fertile mulch that she later spread around the rose bushes in her garden. Now, whenever there is a bloom, it greets her with a tiny 'Hello' and she thinks of her formerly wooden friend.

As for Geppetto, his grand dreams of a puppet companion empire failed to materialise, due to stiff competition from the sexbot industry. He returned to his small village and carved more figures from found and repurposed wood. To stay busy (and to prepare for the possible appearance of another Pinocchio), he performed puppet shows in the village square for the local pre-adults. His most popular show was an update of a classic deemed too violent for modern audiences, which he reinvented as *Listen Supportively and Judy*.

And the individual who happened to be a fairy gave up her efforts for academic tenure. Instead, she assembled a devoted following of volunteers – dolls, mannequins, crash-test dummies and effigies of all kinds – animated both by magick and by progressive ideals. She ran for office and won with a landslide. In a short time, she helped pass consumer fraud legislation (to deal with the fox and the cat), environmental protection statutes (for the whale and the bug) and election reform laws (because, *come on!*). She helped usher in an era of prosperity and fairness, and everyone lived happily ever after, whatever the state of their carbon happened to be.